I LOVE YOU

FOR Miles AND Miles

For Calder, Mabel, and Jonathan —A.G.

ISBN 978-1-338-54274-5

Text copyright © 2017 by Alison Goldberg. Pictures copyright © 2017 by Mike Yamada. All rights reserved. Published by Scholastic Inc., 557 Broadway, New York, NY 10012, by arrangement with Farrar Straus Giroux Books for Young Readers, an imprint of Macmillan Publishing Group, LLC. SCHOLASTIC and associated logos are trademarks and/or registered trademarks of Scholastic Inc.

12 11 10 9 8 7 6 5 4 3 2 1   19 20 21 22 23 24

Printed in the U.S.A.   40

First Scholastic printing, March 2019

Designed by Kristie Radwilowicz

I LOVE YOU
FOR Miles AND Miles

ALISON GOLDBERG   **PICTURES BY MIKE YAMADA**

SCHOLASTIC INC.

My love for you is
Longer than the longest train
Linking engine to caboose,
Winding for miles and miles.

My love for you is
Wider than the widest big rig
Stretching side to side,
Hauling loads of every shape and size.

My love for you is
Stronger than the strongest excavator
Scooping heap after heap,
Lifting with a mighty arm.

My love for you is
Deeper than the deepest drill
Digging down, down, down,
Uncovering mysteries.

My love for you is
Taller than the tallest crane
Rising up, up, up,
Reaching toward the sun.

My love for you is
Smoother than the smoothest sailboat
Skimming wave after wave,
Gliding along.

My love for you is
Faster than the fastest fire truck
Hurrying faster, faster,
Rushing to you, anywhere you are.

My love for you is
Tougher than the toughest tractor
Planting crop after crop,
Helping through mud and muck.

My love for you is
Bigger than the biggest truck
Removing boulders and rocks,
Clearing the way.

My love for you is
Higher than the highest plane
Flying higher, higher,
Soaring above all the rain.

My love for you is
Steadier than the steadiest tugboat
Tugging *puff, puff, puff,*
Guiding you home, day or night.

My love for you is
Longer than the longest train
Riding from station to station,
Traveling with you always.

Alison Goldberg lives with her family in Cambridge, Massachusetts. *I Love You for Miles and Miles* is her debut picture book, inspired by her children's love of all things that go.

Mike Yamada is an illustrator and animation production designer based in Pasadena, California. He has contributed to many animated films, including *How to Train Your Dragon* and *Big Hero 6*, and has illustrated several books for children, such as *Bedtime Blastoff!* by Luke Reynolds and *Kai to the Rescue!* by Audrey Penn.